RUN, EEKI, RUN!

Published by Red Panda, an imprint of Westland Books, a division of Nasadiya Technologies Private Limited, in 2025

No. 269/2B, First Floor, 'Irai Arul', Vimalraj Street, Nethaji Nagar, Alapakkam Main Road, Maduravoyal, Chennai 600095

Westland, the Westland logo, Red Panda and the Red Panda logo are the trademarks of Nasadiya Technologies Private Limited, or its affiliates.

Copyright © Margaret Sood, 2025

Margaret Sood asserts the moral right to be identified as the author of this work.

ISBN: 9789371975520

10 9 8 7 6 5 4 3 2 1

All rights reserved

Book design by Nadia D'souza

Printed at Nutech Print Services Pvt. Ltd

No part of this book may be reproduced, or stored in a retrieval system, or transmitted in any form or by any means, electronic, mechanical, photocopying, recording, or otherwise, without express written permission of the publisher.

emull

He is the **second-largest** bird in the world and looks a bit like an ostrich.

He is also like the ostrich, because he cannot fly.

But that doesn't bother him one bit!

Do you know, he can run—very *fast!*
In fact, he runs all around
my garden trying to catch me.

When I get tired and run into my house,
he runs up to the door.

He peeps inside with his big curious eyes.

He wants to come in but **oh, no!** He **has** to stay out!

And keeps poking his beak at the door.

I have made a little house for him in the garden.

It has straw for a bed and a roof so he doesn't get wet in the rain.

His food is *very strange*.
I guess *he* likes it. But no, not me!

He eats snails, worms, insects,
bits of bread and cookie crumbs ……..
His favourite was an
old cupcake that got **hard**
when I left it in my toy cupboard.

I love to take him for a walk around my neighbourhood.

When I first got my emu,
I named him Eeki.

I tried to teach him tricks,
but I found out something
about emus—they are
not very smart.

He can't fetch a ball
or shake hands like my dog,

And he can't sing
like my bird.

But he can run.
He runs and runs.

So, I guess that is
his special trick.

But I wonder ... how will I take **two** emus for a walk in my neighbourhood?

When I first got my emu,
I named him Eeki.

I tried to teach him tricks,
but I found out something
about emus—they are
not very smart.

He can't fetch a ball
or shake hands like my dog,

And he can't sing
like my bird.

Maybe we'll all just run—
each at our own speed.

Eeki can't fly, fetch or sing, but that's okay.
He's perfect just the way he is.

About the Author

Peggy Sood is currently a curriculum consultant and teacher educator. She served at the American Embassy School, New Delhi, for 30 years as a teacher and Vice Principal. Focusing now on literacy, she conducts workshops for schools and libraries in many cities in India.

She is passionate about developing children's interest in reading and helping adults provide the most appropriate books for them. Her firmly held belief: reading to a child every day is the single greatest predictor of his success in school.

About the Illustrator

Nadia D'Souza is a Goan watercolour artist who paints nature and animals—the purest of all things, bearing the burden of human predicament. Her themes are tinged with satire.